# This First Favourite Tale

## belongs to

_____

Published by Ladybird Books Ltd
27 Wrights Lane London W8 5TZ
A Penguin Company
5 7 9 10 8 6 4

© LADYBIRD BOOKS LTD MCMXCIX

LADYBIRD and the device of a Ladybird are trademarks of Ladybird Books Ltd
All rights reserved. No part of this publication may be reproduced,
stored in a retrieval system, or transmitted in any form or by any
means, electronic, mechanical, photocopying, recording or otherwise,
without the prior consent of the copyright owner.

Printed in Italy

# Jack
## and the
# Beanstalk

BASED ON A TRADITIONAL FOLK TALE

*retold by* Iona Treahy ★ *illustrated by* Ruth Rivers

Once there was a boy called Jack who lived
with his mother. They were so poor that she
said to him one day, "We'll have to sell our
cow – it's the only way."

So Jack took the cow to market.

On the way, Jack met a stranger.

"I'll give you five beans for that cow," she said. "They're magic beans…"

"Done!" said Jack. But when he got back…

"Five beans for our cow?" cried his mother.
And she threw them out of the window.

All through the night, a beanstalk grew… and grew… till it was right out of sight.

Before his mother could say a word, Jack climbed… and climbed… and he didn't stop till he reached…

…the top. There Jack saw a giant castle. He knock-knock-knocked, and a giantess opened the door.

Inside, Jack could hear a **thumping** and a **banging** and a **stamping** and a **crashing**!

What a noise!

"Quick," said the giantess. "Hide!
My husband is hungry!"

"Fee, fi, fo fum! Watch out everyone, HERE I COME!" roared the giant.

The giant sat down for his supper. He ate
a hundred boiled potatoes, and a hundred
chocolate biscuits. And then, feeling a bit
happier, he got out his gold.

The giant started counting his coins,
but soon… he was snoozing.

Jack snatched the gold and *raced* down the beanstalk.

"Gold!" cried Jack's mother when she saw what he'd got. "We're not poor any more!"

But Jack wanted to go back up the beanstalk.
The next day he climbed... and climbed...
and he didn't stop till he reached the top.

Inside the castle, Jack hid when he heard...

It's you again!

a **thumping** and a **banging** and a **stamping** and a **crashing**.

"Fee, fi, fo, fum!
Watch out everyone,
HERE I COME!" roared the giant.

The giant sat down for his supper. He ate two
hundred baked potatoes, and two hundred
jellies. And then, feeling a bit happier, he got
out his hen that laid golden eggs.

The hen started laying, but soon…
the giant was snoozing. Jack snatched
the hen and *raced* down
the beanstalk.

"Golden eggs from a golden hen!"
cried Jack's mother. "Now we'll never
be poor again!"

The next day, Jack climbed the beanstalk
once more.

"Fee, fi, fo, fum!
Watch out everyone,
HERE I COME!" roared the giant.

The giant sat down for his supper. He ate three hundred roast potatoes, and three hundred cream cakes. And then, feeling a bit happier, he got out his silver harp.

The harp sang him lullabies, and soon… the giant was snoozing. Jack snatched the harp and *raced* down the beanstalk.

But the harp called out, "Master! Master!"

The giant woke up and started to chase
after Jack.

"Bring the axe, Mother!" shouted Jack as he neared the ground. Then he chopped and he chopped and he chopped and didn't stop till… CRASH! Down came the beanstalk and the giant.

And with the gold and the harp and the eggs and the hen, Jack and his mother were never poor again.